SUPER CYCLIST

BY

Dave Carl

RED ROVER press

A DIVISION OF THE PUBLISHING CIRCLE

SUPER CYCLIST / DAVE CARL
ISBN: 978-1-947398-60-3 PAPERBACK
ISBN: 978-1-947398-61-0 HARDCOVER

One day on the school playground John saw two boys playing cops and robbers.

He said, "Someday I'm going to fight crime."

One of the boys laughed and pointed at his wheelchair. "Get real. You can't fight crime."

John felt sad,
but he said to himself,
"I don't care what he
says, *I* can do anything!"

John worked out with his handcycle
and grew strong and healthy.

He studied hard to get good grades.

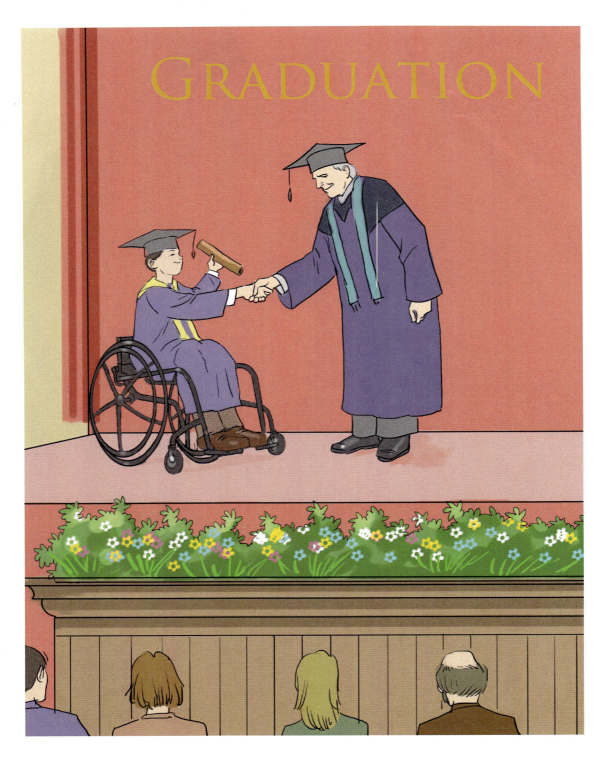

Then he went to college and became a scientist.
He was ready to fight crime.

He thought and thought. "I know. I'll make inventions to help the police."

He poured together some chemicals. He mixed and swirled and experimented. He made a sticky, gooey gel that could stick people to the wall and hold them there until the police came.

"I need a fast way to travel." John thought and worked and fiddled again. He made a super-fast handcycle vehicle.

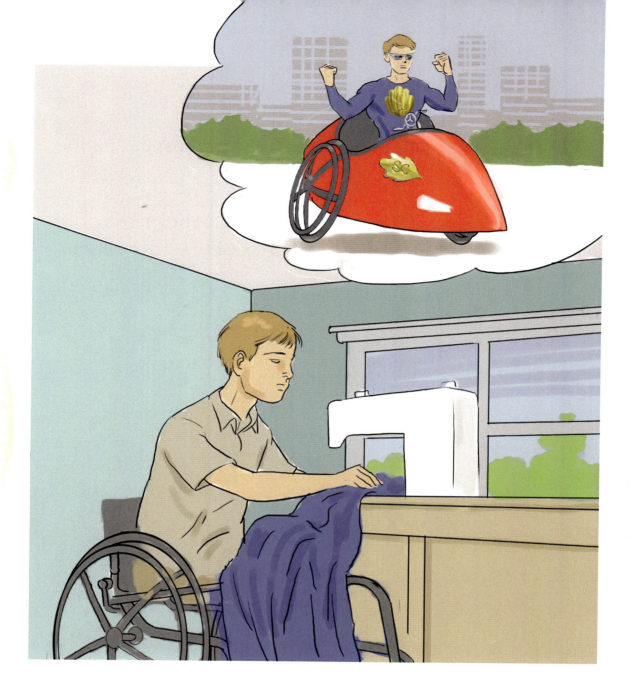

He sewed a special outfit that hid his identity.

"I think I'm ready to fight crime," he said.
"I'll call myself Super Cyclist."

John heard someone yell, "Help! Help!"

He pulled on his crimefighter clothes and popped into his super cycle.

This is a job for Super Cyclist!" he said as he zipped down the street with superhero speed toward the cries.

When he rounded the corner a man yelled,
"They stole my money."

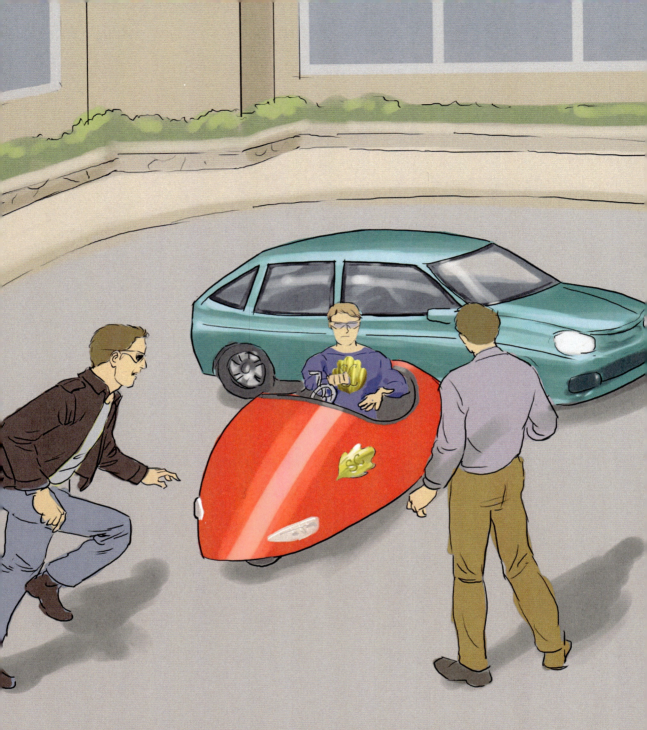

The two thieves ran into Super Cyclist on their way to the getaway car.

Super Cyclist blocked their way and said, "Give the money back and we'll talk."

The robbers pushed his cycle and tried to knock him down. "No way!" they said.

"I warned you!" yelled Super Cyclist.

He threw his special gel at the robbers. It stuck them to the bank's outer wall. Super Cyclist recovered the stolen money, returned it to the bank, then disappeared.

Minutes later, the police arrived. They found the robbers stuck with gel that had the letters SC on it.

"Who did this?" a policeman asked the bank teller.

She said, "It was a super strong man in a special cycle. That's all I know."

The next morning, John heard firetruck sirens.
He changed into Super Cyclist and raced to the
fire. Firefighters were busy putting out the fire.
They didn't see a little girl in the corner window.

Super Cyclist threw a rope up to her window. Because he was so strong from exercising, Super Cyclist climbed up the rope using just his arms.

The girl held onto his neck, and Super Cyclist carried her down and placed her on the ground.

"Thank you. You saved my life," she said.

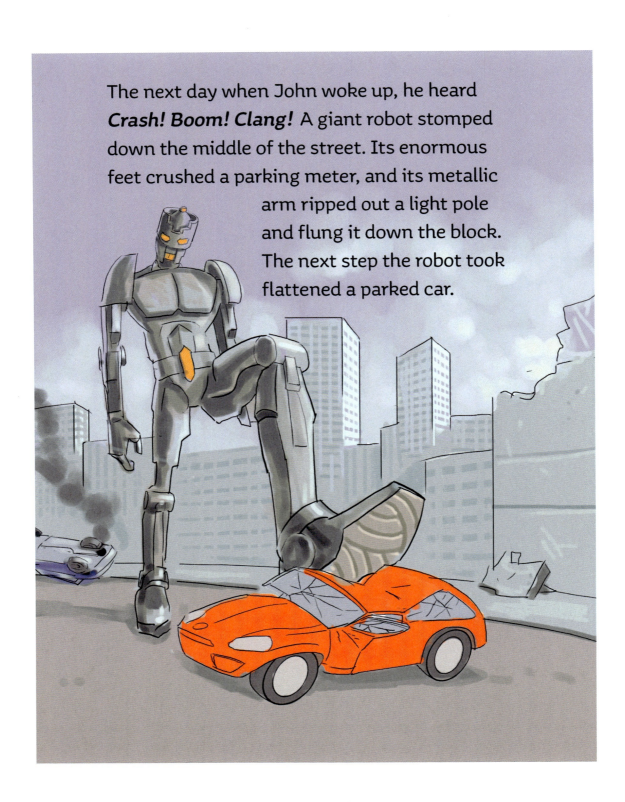

The next day when John woke up, he heard **Crash! Boom! Clang!** A giant robot stomped down the middle of the street. Its enormous feet crushed a parking meter, and its metallic arm ripped out a light pole and flung it down the block. The next step the robot took flattened a parked car.

"Hey, look over here!"
Super Cyclist called.

The robot
turned
toward him.

Super Cyclist raced to the robot and threw super gel
at its arms. The gel stuck the robot's arms together.
The robot growled and yanked and yanked against
the goo until finally freeing his arms.
It then reached down and snatched
Super Cyclist, throwing
him against the building.
The robot turned and
marched away.

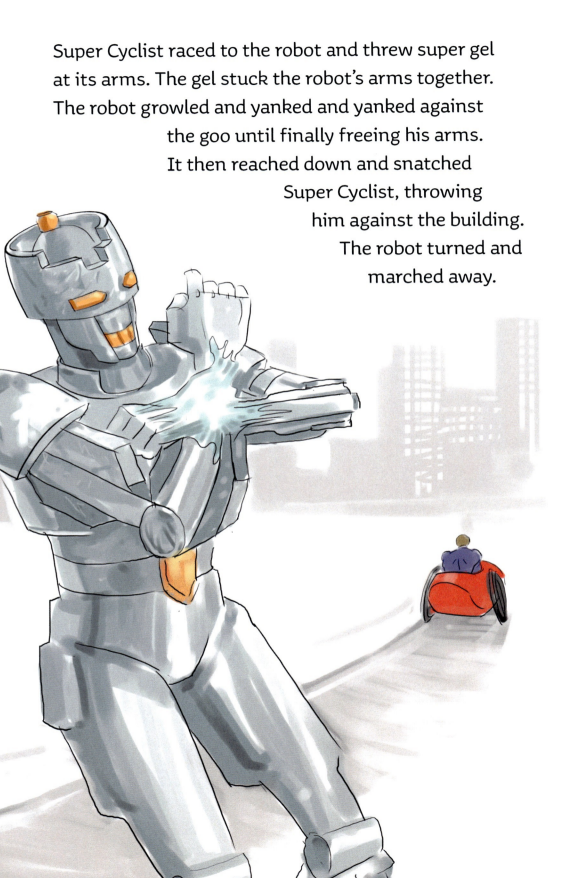

Super Cyclist drug himself back to his cycle.
He was running out of time to save the city!

The robot marched on to City Hall. He smashed through the building and grabbed Mayor Jones.

"Help me! Mayor Jones yelled. "Do something!" But everyone ran away . . . everyone but Super Cyclist.

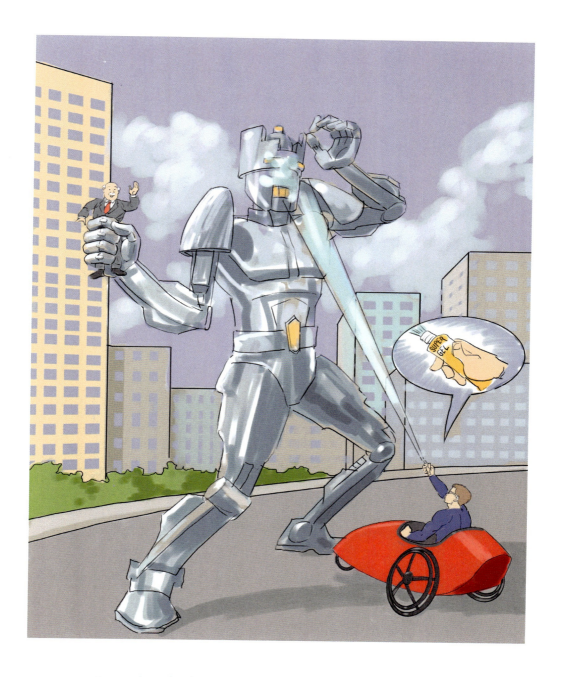

He wheeled close to the robot and threw
super gel at the robot's face. It couldn't see.
Super Cyclist wrapped his rope around the
robot's feet and yanked.

The robot fell over and Mayor Jones escaped.

The mayor turned to Super Cyclist to thank him.

It was then Super Cyclist suddenly realized the man was the boy who once belittled him and his wheelchair, insisting there was no way John could ever fight crime.

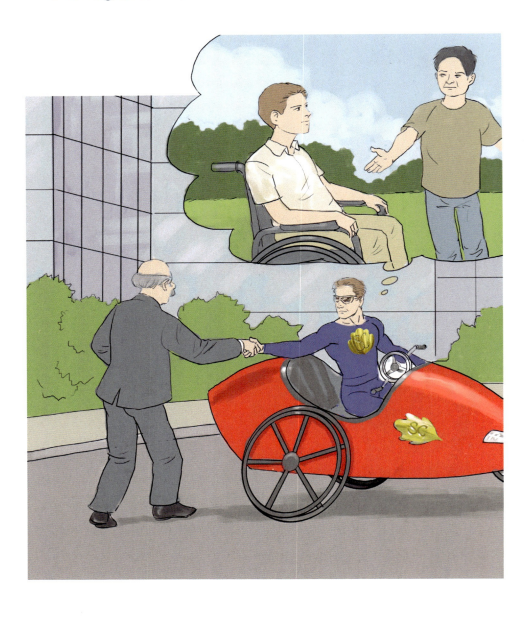

"I don't know how we can thank you," the mayor said.
"Our city owes you so much!"

"No need for thanks," said Super Cyclist.
"Just remember, when danger is in the air,
Super Cyclist **will** be there!"

And with that he spun away
toward his next adventure.

Dave Carl is the creative mind behind *Super Cyclist*, and is available to speak at schools, corporations, and seminars. His inspirational talks encourage adults and kids to believe in themselves so that they can reach their goals—to be *all* that they can be.

www.supercyclist.com
DaveAC12@gmail.com

Born with spina bifida, a condition where the spinal cord doesn't fully develop, Dave Carl is paralyzed from the waist down. But he has never let his disability define or limit him. He earned a bachelor's degree in Social Work from Buffalo State College, and now gives back to his community in huge ways—through his job, and as a motivational speaker, author, blogger, and volunteer.

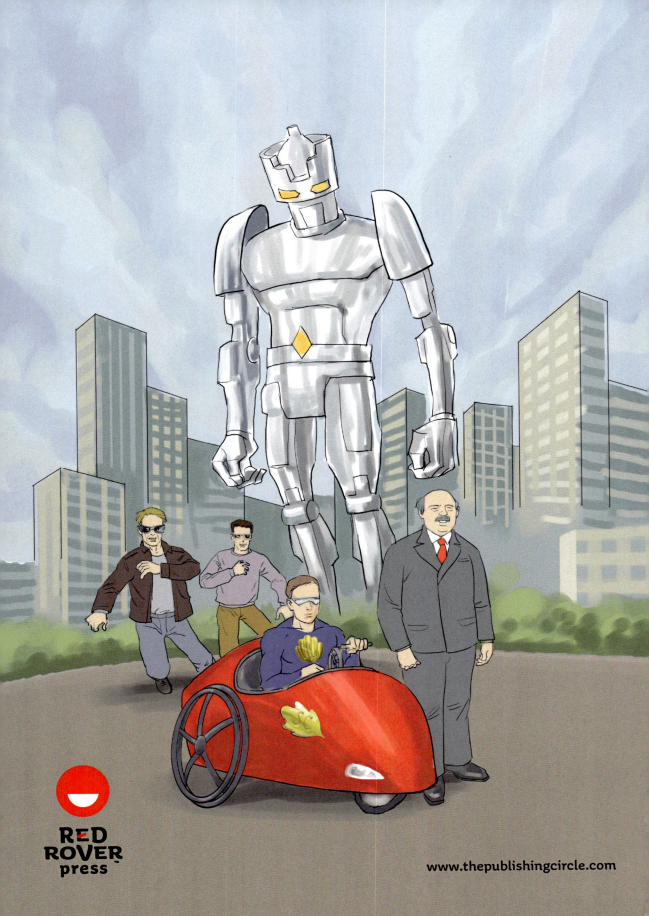

www.thepublishingcircle.com